Twas the Night Before Christmas

Twas the Night Before Christmas
A Visit from St. Nicholas

By Clement C. Moore

Illustrated by Jessie Willcox Smith

Derrydale Books
New York · Avenel, New Jersey

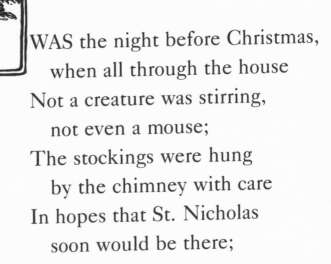

'TWAS the night before Christmas,
   when all through the house
Not a creature was stirring,
   not even a mouse;
The stockings were hung
   by the chimney with care
In hopes that St. Nicholas
   soon would be there;

THE children were nestled
  all snug in their beds,
While visions of sugar plums
  danced in their heads;
And Mamma in her kerchief,
  and I in my cap,
Had just settled our brains
  for a long winter's nap,

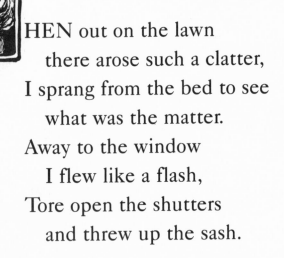

WHEN out on the lawn
 there arose such a clatter,
I sprang from the bed to see
 what was the matter.
Away to the window
 I flew like a flash,
Tore open the shutters
 and threw up the sash.

HE moon on the breast
   of the new-fallen snow
Gave the luster of midday
   to objects below,
When, what to my wondering
   eyes should appear,
But a miniature sleigh,
   and eight tiny reindeer,

ITH a little old driver,
    so lively and quick,
I knew in a moment
    it must be St. Nick.
More rapid than eagles
    his coursers they came,
And he whistled, and shouted,
    and called them by name:

OW, Dasher! Now, Dancer!
 Now, Prancer and Vixen!
On, Comet! On, Cupid!
 On, Donder and Blitzen!
To the top of the porch,
 to the top of the wall,
Now dash away, dash away,
 dash away all!''

JESSIE WILLCOX SMITH.

S dry leaves that before
   the wild hurricane fly,
When they meet with an obstacle,
   mount to the sky;
So up to the housetop
   the coursers they flew,
With the sleigh full of toys,
   and St. Nicholas too.

ND then, in a twinkling,
   I heard on the roof
The prancing and pawing
   of each little hoof.
As I drew in my head,
   and was turning around,
Down the chimney St. Nicholas
   came with a bound.

E was dressed all in fur,
  from his head to his foot,
And his clothes were all tarnished
  with ashes and soot;
A bundle of toys
  he had flung on his back,
And he looked like a peddler
  just opening his pack.

IS eyes—how they twinkled!
His dimples, how merry!
His cheeks were like roses,
his nose like a cherry!
His droll little mouth
was drawn up like a bow,
And the beard of his chin
was as white as the snow.

HE stump of a pipe
   he held tight in his teeth,
And the smoke it encircled
   his head like a wreath;
He had a broad face
   and a little round belly,
That shook when he laughed,
   like a bowlful of jelly.

E was chubby and plump,
  a right jolly old elf,
And I laughed when I saw him,
  in spite of myself;
A wink of his eye
  and a twist of his head,
Soon gave me to know
  I had nothing to dread;

E spoke not a word,
   but went straight to his work,
And filled all the stockings;
   then turned with a jerk,
And laying his finger
   aside of his nose,
And giving a nod,
   up the chimney he rose;

E sprang to his sleigh,
  to his team gave a whistle,
And away they all flew
  like the down of a thistle.
But I heard him exclaim,
  ere he drove out of sight,
*"Happy Christmas to all,
  and to all a good night."*

ABOUT THE POEM

MID many celebrations last Christmas Eve, in various places by different persons, there was one, in New York City, not like any other anywhere. A company of men, women, and children went together just after the evening service in their church, and, standing around the tomb of the author of "A Visit from St. Nicholas," recited together the words of the poem which we all know so well and love so dearly.

Dr. Clement C. Moore, who wrote the poem, never expected that he would be remembered by it. If he expected to be famous at all as a writer, he thought it would be because of the Hebrew Dictionary that he wrote.

He was born in a house near Chelsea Square, New York City, in 1781; and he lived there all his life. It was a great big house, with fireplaces in it; just the house to be living in on Christmas Eve.

Dr. Moore had children. He liked writing poetry for them even more than he liked writing a Hebrew Dictionary. He wrote a whole book of poems for them.

One year he wrote this poem, which we usually call "Twas the Night before Christmas," to give to his children for a Christmas present. They read it just after they had hung up their stockings before one of the big fireplaces in their house. Afterward, they learned it, and sometimes recited it, just as other children learn it and recite it now.

It was printed in a newspaper. Then a magazine printed it, and after a time it was printed in the school readers. Later it was printed by itself, with pictures. Then it was translated into German, French, and many other languages. It was even made into Braille, which is the raised printing that blind children read with their fingers. But never has it been given to us in so attractive a form as in this book. It has happened that almost all the children in the world know this poem. How few of them know any Hebrew!

Every Christmas Eve the young men studying to be ministers at the General Theological Seminary, New York City, put a holly wreath around Dr. Moore's picture, which is on the wall of their dining room. Why? Because he gave the ground on which the General Theological Seminary stands? Because he wrote a Hebrew Dictionary? No. They do it because he was the author of "A Visit from St. Nicholas."

Most of the children probably know the words of the poem. They are old. But the pictures that Miss Jessie Willcox Smith has painted for this edition of it are new. All the children, probably, have seen other pictures painted by Miss Smith, showing children at other seasons of the year. How much they will enjoy looking at these pictures, showing children on that night that children like best — Christmas Eve!

E. McC.

1912

This 1992 edition is published by Derrydale Books,
distributed by Outlet Book Company, a Random House Company,
40 Engelhard Avenue, Avenel, New Jersey 07001.

Printed and bound in the United States of America

Library of Congress Cataloging-in-Publication Data
Moore, Clement Clarke, 1779–1863.
[Night before Christmas]
'Twas the night before Christmas / by Clement C. Moore ;
illustrated by Jessie Willcox Smith.
p.   cm.
Known under title: The night before Christmas.
Summary: The well-known poem about an important Christmas visitor.
ISBN 0-517-08136-9
1. Santa Claus—Juvenile poetry.   2. Christmas—Juvenile poetry.
3. Children's poetry, American.   [1. Santa Claus—Poetry.
2. Christmas—Poetry.   3. American poetry.   4. Narrative poetry.]
I. Smith, Jessie Willcox, 1863–1935, ill.   II. Title.
PS2429.M5N5   1992c
811'.2—dc20   92-10726
                                                   CIP
                                                   AC

For this edition of Twas the Night Before Christmas:
Cover design: Clair Moritz
Production supervisor: Susan Wein
Editorial supervision: Claire Booss

8 7 6 5 4 3 2 1